You Loves Ewe!

story, pictures, and wacky wordplay by CECE BELL

CLARION BOOKS
Houghton Mifflin Harcourt
Boston New York

For my sister, Sarah,
and for all my pals named
Sarah (or Sara)

Clarion Books, 3 Park Avenue, New York, New York 10016 • Copyright © 2019 by Cece Bell
All rights reserved. • For information about permission to reproduce selections from this book,
write to trade.permissions@hmhco.com or to Permissions, Houghton Mifflin Harcourt
Publishing Company, 3 Park Avenue, 19th Floor, New York, New York 10016. • Clarion Books
is an imprint of Houghton Mifflin Harcourt Publishing Company. • hmhbooks.com • The
illustrations in this book were done in china marker and acrylics on vellum. • The text
was set in ITC American Typewriter Std Medium. • Library of Congress Cataloging-
in-Publication Data • Names: Bell, Cece, author, illustrator. • Title: You loves Ewe! /
story, pictures, and wacky wordplay by Cece Bell. • Description: Boston ; New York :
Clarion Books, Houghton Mifflin Harcourt, [2019] • Summary: Homonyms cause
great confusion as an increasingly cranky yam tries to make introductions and
provide explanations to a newly-arrived and rather silly donkey. • Identifiers: LCCN
2018052003 ISBN 9781328526113 (hardcover picture book) • Subjects: CYAC:
English language—Homonyms—Fiction. • Donkeys—Fiction • Yams—Fiction. • Sheep—
Fiction. • Humorous stories. • Classification: LCC PZ7.B38891527 You 2019
DDC [E]—dc23 • LC record available at https://lccn.loc.gov/2018052003
Manufactured in China • SCP 10 9 8 7 6 5 4 3 2 1 • 4500771605

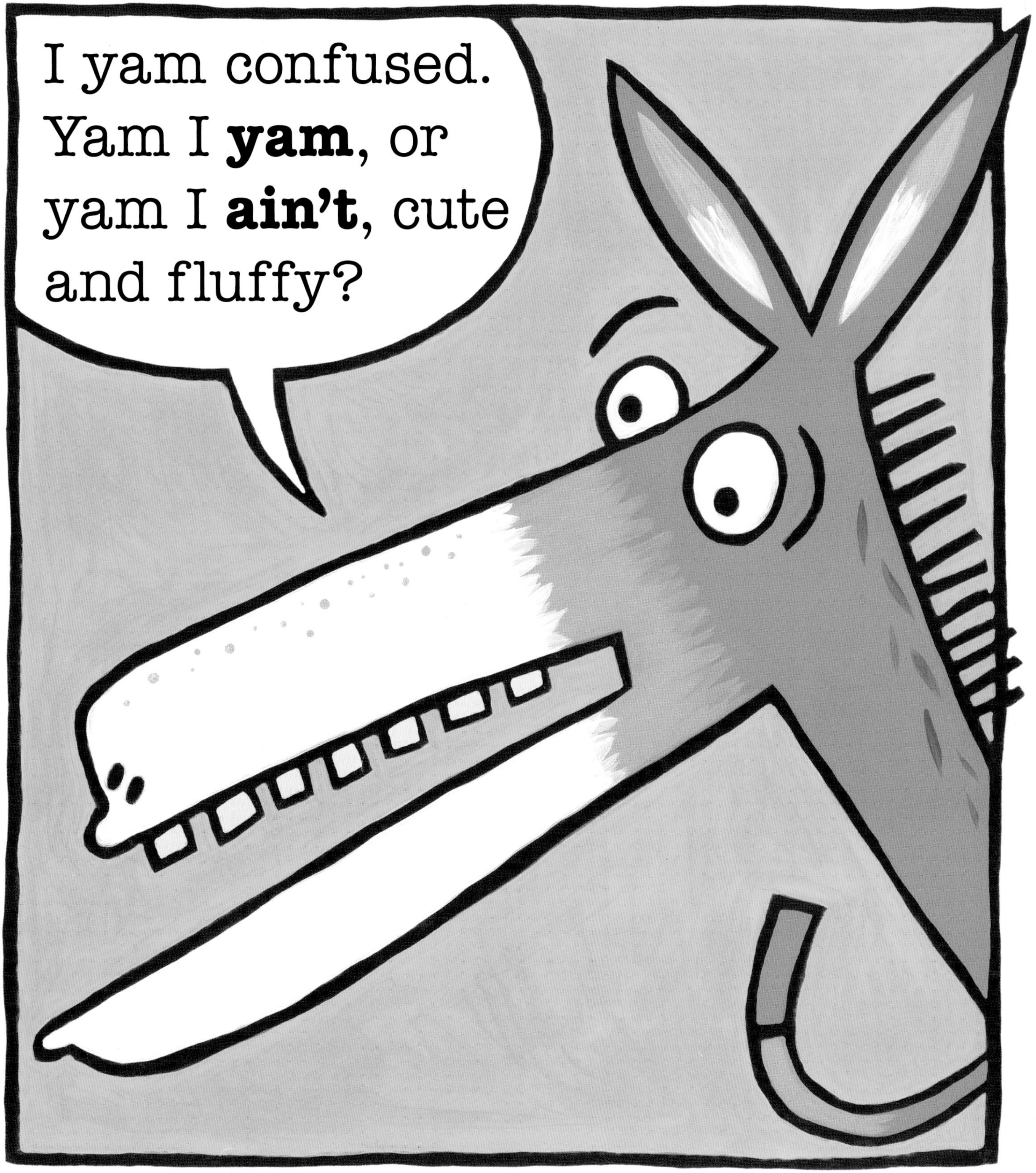
I yam confused. Yam I **yam**, or yam I **ain't**, cute and fluffy?

But wait—